Tommy
Starts Something
Big:

Giving Cuddles
with Kindness

By Chuck Gaidica
with Kris Yankee
Illustrated by Mary Gregg Byrne

FERNE PRESS

Tommy Starts Something Big: Giving Cuddles with Kindness
Copyright © 2011 by Chuck Gaidica
Illustrated by Mary Gregg Byrne
Layout and cover design by Kimberly Franzen
Illustrations created with watercolors.
Printed in the United States of America

Summary: After six-year-old Tommy receives a special teddy bear from his aunt, he realizes that everyone should have a cuddle bear of their own.

Library of Congress Cataloging-in-Publication Data
Gaidica, Chuck
Tommy Starts Something Big: Giving Cuddles with Kindness/Chuck Gaidica with Kris Yankee–First Edition
ISBN-13: 978-1-933916-76-7
1. Juvenile fiction. 2. Teddy bears. 3. Cuddling.
I. Yankee, Kris II. Tommy Starts Something Big: Giving Cuddles with Kindness
Library of Congress Control Number: 2010939917

FERNE PRESS

Ferne Press is an imprint of Nelson Publishing & Marketing
366 Welch Road, Northville, MI 48167
www.nelsonpublishingandmarketing.com
(248) 735-0418

I dedicate this book to my five children and my loving wife, Susan.
Thanks for all the cuddles and for always supporting me.

Many thanks to writer Kris Yankee, publisher Marian Nelson, and
illustrator Mary Gregg Byrne for being part of the Cuddle Alert team.
With their help, Tommy and his family have come to life and reminded all
of us that we are never too young or too small to start something big!

"Thanks for the bear, Aunt Suzi," Tommy said.

"This bear is stuffed with extra-special cuddly love," Aunt Suzi replied.

"Wow! He's pretty soft. He's gonna go next to my pillow."

"Great. That's exactly why I made him for you," Aunt Suzi said, and she gave him a big hug.

After dinner, Tommy was riding his bike. He hit a big rock and fell hard.

"Owww!" Tommy cried. "It really hurts!"

His friend Darnelle yelled, "I'll get your mom!"

When ambulance driver Marc arrived, he said, "That might be a broken leg, Mom. We should take him to the hospital."

"This stinks getting hurt on my birthday," Tommy said.

"We're going to take an ambulance ride," Mom said. "Here, cuddle with your bear. He'll help."

"I do feel better having Cuddles."

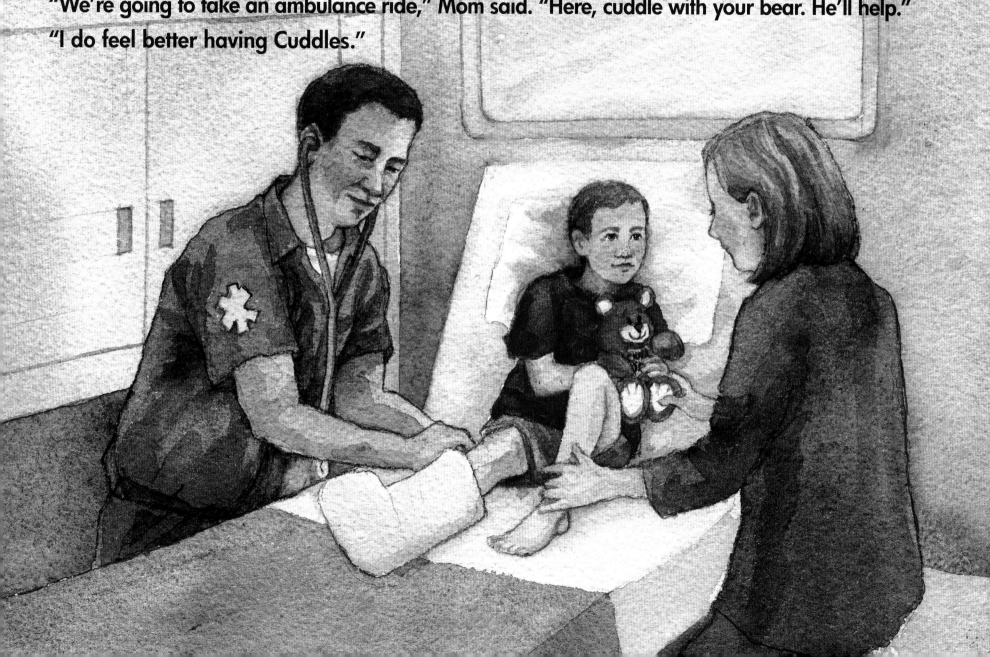

"Have you ever had a cast, Tommy?" the doctor asked.

"No. Will it hurt?"

"Not really. Your leg probably hurts more now. After the cast is on, your leg will just be itchy."

"You must be special," Tommy said to Cuddles, "'cuz my leg doesn't hurt much."

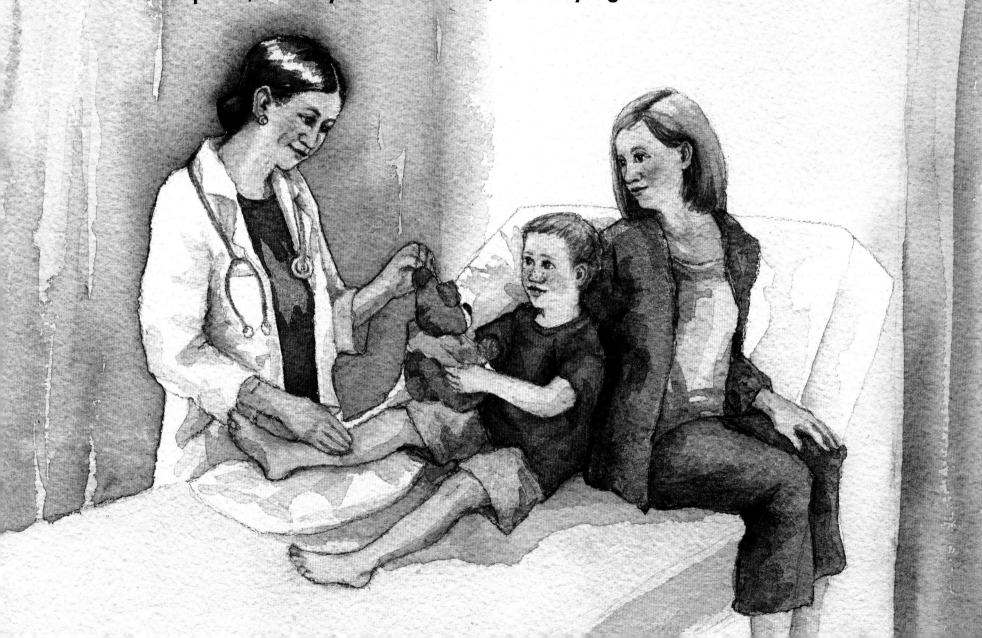

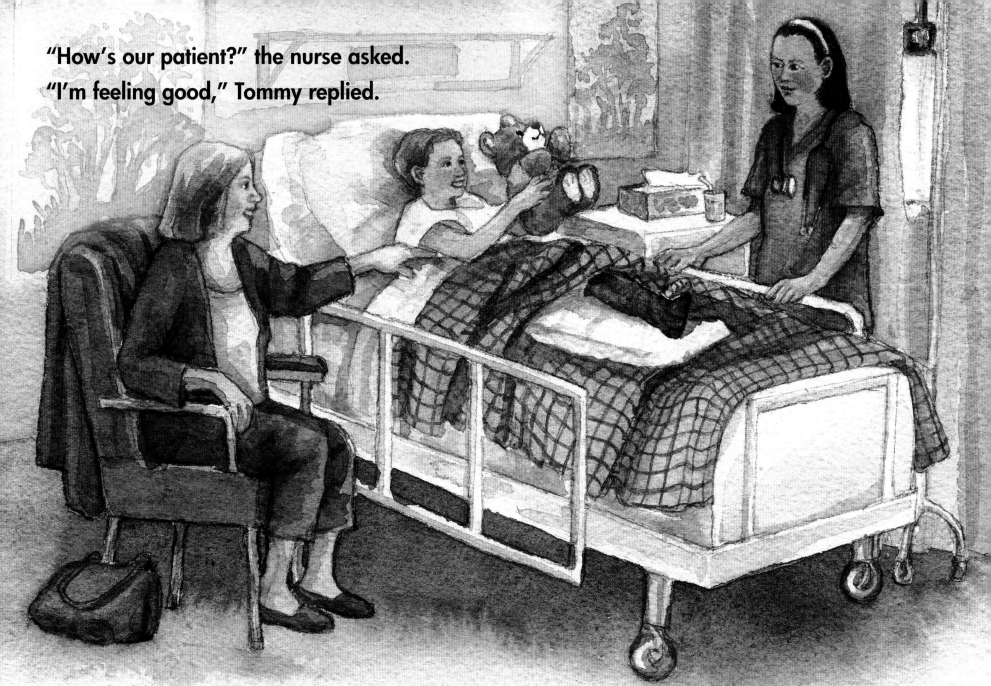

"How's our patient?" the nurse asked.

"I'm feeling good," Tommy replied.

"Your bear is awfully cute," the nurse said. "You have to stay here overnight. I hope that doesn't make you too sad."

"That's okay. I have Cuddles. He helps me feel safe."

Before leaving the hospital, Mom took Tommy and Cuddles to the cafeteria for an ice cream treat.

"Hi, Marc!" Tommy said. "See my cast?"

"That's a great color, kiddo. And, I really like your bear."

Marc's walkie-talkie beeped. "Duty calls," Marc said as he waved goodbye.

"I wonder if Marc's gonna rescue somebody who needs a cuddle bear," Tommy said. "Wow, look at all the people here visiting their families who need Cuddles."

On the way home, Mom said, "You're so quiet. What are you thinking about?"
"All those people who don't have Cuddles. I bet they're sad."

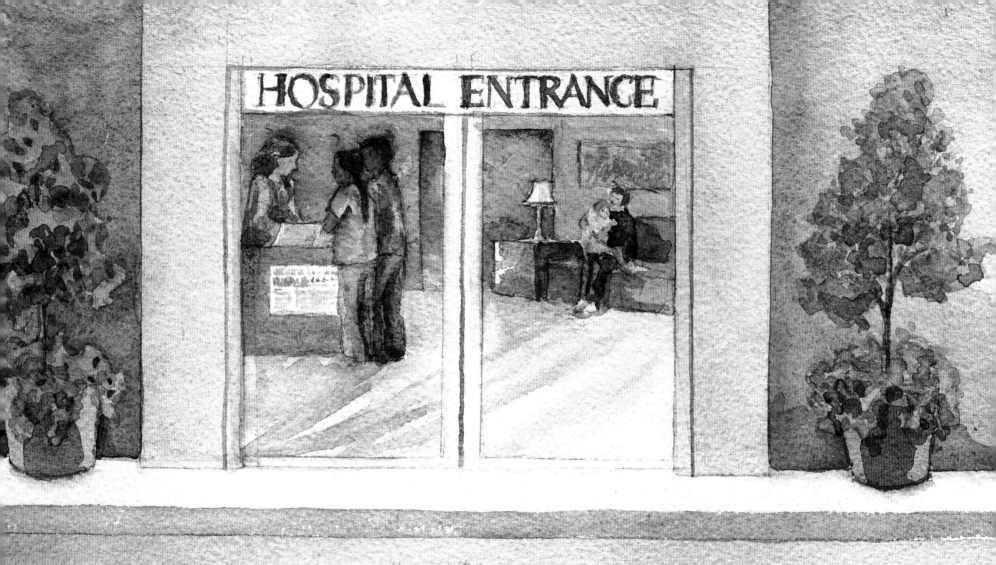

"Do you think Aunt Suzi can make more bears?" Tommy asked.

"We can call her and ask."

"I'll help, too!" Tommy laughed. "It'll be fun."

The next morning, Aunt Suzi brought the materials to make more cuddle bears.

"Stuff them like this, Tommy," Aunt Suzi instructed. "Wait. One more thing, we have to give him some love so he can give love to others."

When the bears were finished, Tommy lined them up.

"Who gets all these bears?" Mom asked.

"We'll know when we see someone who needs a cuddle alert," Tommy said. "Can we go back to the hospital?"

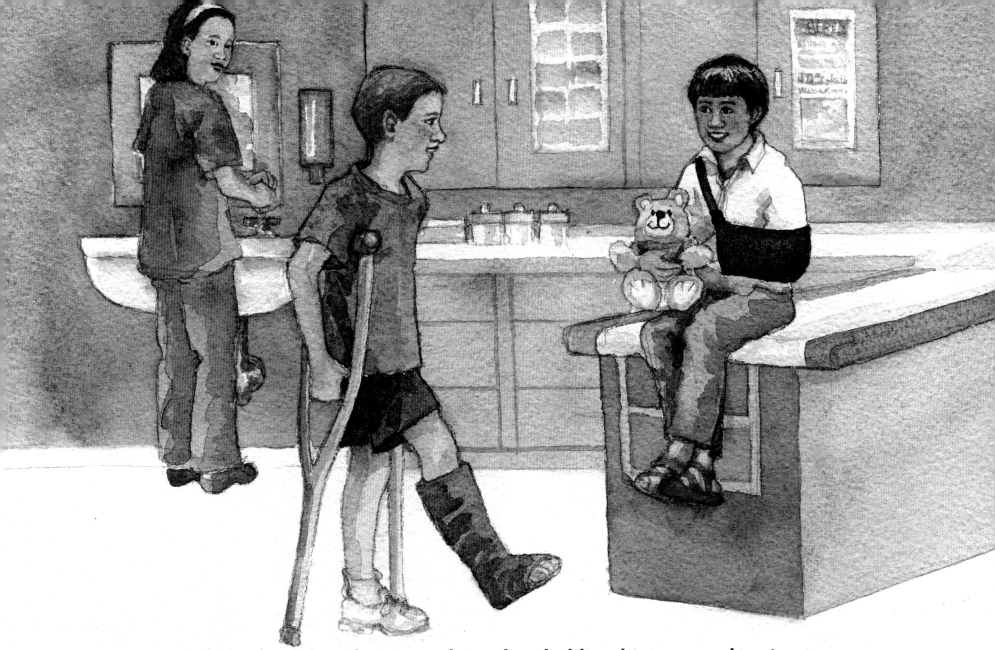

"Cuddle alert!" Tommy said, as he pointed to a boy holding his arm and crying.

"You look like you need a cuddle bear," Tommy said. "It won't be so scary when you see the doctor."

"How do you know?" the boy asked.

"I know."

"Another cuddle alert! Look, my nurse."

"Hi, Tommy. How's the leg?"

"It's great, Nurse Tina. I brought a special bear just for you. And, here's another one. You decide who needs this bear."

"Thank you," Nurse Tina said as she hugged her bear. "He's extra soft. I love him."

"Cuddle alert!" Tommy said. "Hey, Marc."

"Hey, kiddo," Marc said.

"This cuddle bear is for you."

Marc nuzzled his bear and said, "Thanks. I could really use more of these for other kids."

"Can we make more, Mom?"

"Of course."

"Where should we go next?" Aunt Suzi asked.

"Can we visit Nana?"

MERGENCY

"Great idea. Nana would love to see you and meet Cuddles," Mom replied.

"Cuddle alert! Hi, Nana!"

"There's my sweetheart," Nana said. "Do you still get to play outside with your friends even though you have crutches?"

"No," Tommy replied, "but Cuddles doesn't let me get lonely. I've brought one for you, too."

"His extra-special love will keep you from getting lonely. And see his arms?" Tommy asked. "They're long so he can hug you back."

Nana cuddled with her bear and sighed. "I'll never be lonely now that I have my own cuddle bear."

After they said their goodbyes to Nana, the three went home to have lunch. The mailman was just walking down their driveway.

"Is that another cuddle alert, Tommy?" Aunt Suzi asked.

"I think so. Look how hard he works."

"Hi, Mr. McCreadie," Tommy said. "Your load looks extra heavy today. Do you have room for one of my cuddle bears?"

"Why do I need a bear?" Mr. McCreadie asked.

"He'll keep you company all day long."

"Thank you. He'll ride with me in my bag."

After lunch, Tommy and Mom sat in their front yard.

"Do you think she's a cuddle alert?" Mom asked, pointing to the girl near a moving truck.

"She doesn't look very happy."

"It's hard moving into a new neighborhood, remember?" Mom asked.

"I think she needs a cuddle bear."

"Hi. My name's Tommy."

"Hi. I'm Solena."

"You're new here," Tommy said.

"Yep, we just moved in."

"When we moved, I was sad to leave my friends. And, it was scary going to a new school."

"That's how I feel," Solena said.

"Here. You need this," Tommy said.

"You're right! Now I've got two new friends."
"Do you think I could have one for my little brother?"
"Sure," Tommy said. "I'll go get one. Hey, Mom!"

Later that night, Dad tucked Tommy into bed.

"I heard you, Mom, and Aunt Suzi had quite a day," Dad said.

"We sure did. There are lots of people who need Cuddles."

"I'm very proud of you." Dad reached into his pocket and took out a coin.

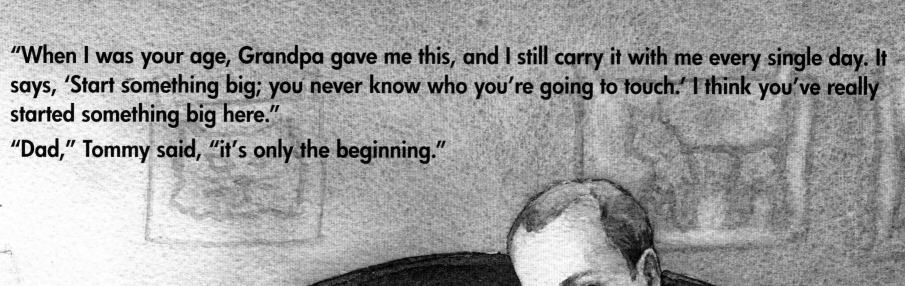

"When I was your age, Grandpa gave me this, and I still carry it with me every single day. It says, 'Start something big; you never know who you're going to touch.' I think you've really started something big here."

"Dad," Tommy said, "it's only the beginning."

It was near the beginning of my TV weather forecasting career in Little Rock, Arkansas, when I decided to create a fun phrase to describe unusually cold nights. The "Cuddle Alert" was born. A "Cuddle Alert" is a call to action to cuddle with somebody or something to stay warm.

This fun phrase started to take on a new meaning as I researched the idea of cuddling and hugging. I discovered the healthful and positive results of offering somebody a hug or a stuffed bear to cuddle. The idea for this children's book grew out of a movement to provide "cuddle bears" to children experiencing a crisis, trauma, or tragedy. Eventually nearly eight thousand cuddle bears were given away to firefighters and first responders who were instructed to give them away to kids in need.

My intent with this children's book is to explore the concept of reaching out to others in a whole new way.

~Chuck

Chuck Gaidica is an Emmy Award–winning television and radio personality in Detroit, Michigan. Chuck currently works as the Director of Meteorology at WDIV-TV and is co-host of the morning radio show at WOMC-FM. Chuck has also been seen on NBC's *Today Show* issuing a "Cuddle Alert" nationally and is a frequent speaker in the Detroit metro area.

Chuck and his wife, Susan, have five children and live in Northville, Michigan. They love their family and their dogs. They have a rich church life and a deep relationship with God.

A portion of the proceeds from all of Chuck's projects will benefit charity.

For more information, visit www.cuddlealert.com.

Kris Yankee is a writer of middle-grade chapter books and women's fiction, as well as a freelance editor. She lives with her husband, two boys, and their dog, Jack, in Southeastern Michigan. To learn more about Kris and her projects, please visit www.krisyankee.com.

Mary Gregg Byrne lives in Bellingham, Washington. She reads, writes, and creates art. Mary teaches watercolor classes and illustrates children's books. She watches her garden and the children grow. She walks in the mountains. She cherishes her friends. Mary enjoys the changing light of the seasons and of her life. For more information about Mary and her art, please visit www.marygreggbyrne.com.

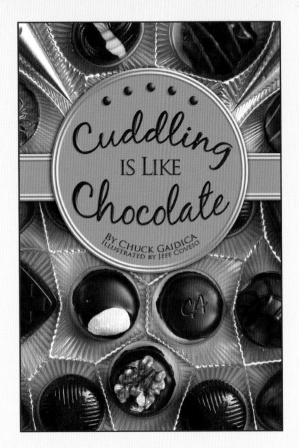

Also by Chuck Gaidica,
Cuddling is Like Chocolate.
www.cuddlealert.com